Daramad of Chahargah: A Study in the Performance Practice of Persian Music

Daramad of Chahargah: A Study in the Performance Practice of Persian Music

Bruno Nettl
with Bela Foltin, Jr.

Information Coordinators, Inc.

Copyright 1972 by Bruno Nettl
Printed and bound in the United States of America
Price $6.00
Library of Congress Catalog Card Number: 74-175174
Standard Book Number: 911772

Information Coordinators, Inc.
1435-37 Randolph Street
Detroit, Michigan 48226

CONTENTS

To

PROFESSOR NOUR-ALI BORUMAND

ACKNOWLEDGMENTS

THIS STUDY is the result of research carried out during the years 1968-1970. Most of the information was gathered, and the recordings made, by myself in Iran in 1968 and 1969. The field research was made possible largely by a Fulbright grant from the U.S. Commission for Cultural Exchange with Iran. Additional support was provided by the University of Illinois Research Board, and by the Center for International Comparative Studies of the University of Illinois. I should like to express my gratitude to all of these institutions. This study may be regarded as a contribution to a major project, entitled "The Maqam Tradition in Theory and Practice: a Comparative Study of Factors Affecting the Deployment and Change of a Musical Tradition," a project which will result in several publications by a number of collaborators under the leadership of Alexander L. Ringer.

Mr. Foltin's role in this project has been largely that of a research assistant, who was responsible in large measure for making transcriptions and analyses of the recorded material. His participation was made possible by a grant from the University of Illinois Research Board.

Inasmuch as this is a discussion, sometimes a critical one, of performances by a number of living musicians, it appeared proper not to mention them by name, but, instead, to number the performances and to give some relevant background information about each performer. I should like to express my gratitude to all of the masters of Persian music with whom I worked for making the recordings for me, and for their patience and forbearance in the face of a naive foreigner who wished to know all sorts of unusual things for inexplicable reasons. In particular, I should like to mention by name my main teacher and mentor in Persian music, Dr. Nour-Ali Borumand, without whose patient instruction I would have found it impossible to gain even the most preliminary insight into Persian music. I must also express my gratitude to three Iranian musicologists, Dr. Mehdi Barkechli, Dr. Hormoz Farhat and Dr. Mohammed Massudieh, for their kind advice and their help in making contacts with musicians, and to Professor William Kay Archer, Director of the Tehran Research Unit of the University of Illinois and the University of Tehran, for many kinds of help.

The recordings from Khorasan were made by myself in conjunction with Mr. Stephen Blum, then a graduate student at the University of Illinois, or by Mr. Blum himself. I am indebted to Mr. Blum for his help and his participation in this project.

The recordings on which this study is based are deposited in the Archives of Ethnomusicology, University of Illinois at Urbana-Champaign.

B. N.

9

INTRODUCTION

MUCH OF the art music of the Middle East and South Asia is said to be improvised. In some respects, this is also true of the art or classical music of Iran, as it was practiced in the 1960's. The nature of this improvisation, usually seen as based on traditional pre-existing materials and musical concepts, i. e. raga, dastgāh, maqam, has been investigated in a number of publications. Indeed, the system of dastgāhā in Persian music has been explicated in several parallel publications, [1] by Farhat, [2] Zonis, [3] Caron and Safvate, [4] Gerson-Kiwi, [5] and Khatchi. [6] The need for more detailed investigation of improvisation and performance practices was evidently felt by Massudieh, [7] who provided a study based upon a very limited number of performances of the dastgāh of shur, and Wilkens, [8] who compared recordings of two musicians.

The purpose of this study is to attempt a contribution to the understanding of Persian improvisation from a point of view somewhat different from those used in the above publications. It is based upon a collection of over forty performances, most of them recorded in the field, of one dastgāh, or mode, chahārgāh. These recordings have been analyzed and serve as the basis of a comparative study. The object is to illustrate some of the ways in which the same material is performed by various musicians in contemporary performance practice, or, to state it differently, in which a single model is interpreted by different musicians. We will be concerned primarily with the introductory section, or darāmad of chahārgāh, a section which also is the most characteristic part of this dastgāh.

The procedure is essentially descriptive of the range of materials subsumed under the concept of darāmad of chahārgāh. Emphasis is upon the structural aspects of the performances. We have attempted mainly to deal with thematic content, sectioning, and the building of intensity, but little with the details of rhythm and ornamentation, areas that evidently do not contribute as much to an understanding of the variety among the performances found in Persian music or of the differences among performances and performers. It may be hoped that additional descriptions of other dastgāhā, their constituent gushehā, and performer groups will follow, so that eventually there will be available a broad body of materials making possible studies as detailed as we now have for aspects of the history of European art music.

The concept of improvisation as such may be questioned in terms of its usefulness for providing insight into the nature of Persian music. But retaining it for the moment, it must first be pointed out that a great deal of Persian art music is not improvised, but consists of pieces that are said to be composed, and to be performed precisely the same way each time. Among these are introductory metric pieces (pishdarāmad), songs (usually tasnif), dances (reng), and pieces with technical virtuosity (chahār mezrāb). At the other

11

end of the spectrum is the type of performance called āvāz (literally, "song" or "singing"), in which the performer's contribution is greatest, and to which the concept of improvisation may be applied. There are several intermediate types of material, which are essentially metric pieces that can be performed with considerable freedom. The composed pieces have, in their structure, many of the characteristics that are also found in the improvisations: repetition, variation of a motif, extension, sequence, reliance on tetrachords. Thus, the traditional division between "composed" and "improvised" materials in Persian music may have limited value.

This view is reinforced and becomes more relevant when we examine the attitudes of musicians. The ones who were asked about the concept of improvisation had very considerably different reactions to it. Those who had been in contact with western musicians and with western ways of thinking about music were familiar with the concept and accepted it readily. Others, however, were somewhat baffled by it. For example, one young violinist (who performed Persian as well as western music), when asked to make a second recording of chahārgāh, asked why I wanted it, since he had already made one for me. Upon being told that his performance was, after all, different each time, he maintained that this was not so, but rather that he played chahārgāh the same way on every occasion. When confronted with objective evidence of the differences in performances, he retreated, saying that they resulted from changes in his mood. In general, while qualitative differences among performers were recognized and even emphasized by musicians, these differences were said mainly to involve technical proficiency, extent of repertory, and knowledge of the fundamental canon of material upon which performances and improvisations are based, known as the radif. The concept of creativity in improvisation was not frequently mentioned as an important distinguishing feature of musicians. It appears that the concept of improvisation as traditionally defined is, at least now, not really used in Persian musical culture.

Possibly, then, it may also turn out not to be useful, at least without critical examination, in an outsider's analysis of the music. Already we have stated that some of the structural characteristics of the "composed" portions of the music are also found in the "improvised" portions. Someone not acquainted with the dichotomy might not find, through analysis, any essential difference between the two kinds of performance. Moreover, there are portions of music which occupy a sort of middle ground between "improvised" and composed pieces.

One of the most important obstacles to the unfettered use of the term, improvisation, for Persian music is the absence of a clear, learned model on which a musician bases his performance. In contrast to jazz (in which a specific series of chords or a popular tune, either of which can be performed in isolation, is the basis of improvisation), there is difficulty in isolating

12

models upon which improvisation is based. That models exist we must take for granted. But they seem -- unless one considers the "teaching versions" which students learn from their teachers and memorize -- hardly to be accessible in audible form. In view of all of these considerations, it seems wisest to regard this study not one of improvisation but rather one of performance practices.

The musical cultures or repertories in which improvisation is used may be viewed as parts of a continuum in the relationship between the composer (or a traditional model, when the creator is unknown), and the performer. Both extremes of the continuum are found in western art music, one in the extremely precise directions to performers in the nineteenth and some twentieth century music and in the attitude that conformance to the composer's intentions is of great importance, and the other, in the creations of the freely improvising ensembles of avant-garde musicians. Outside western civilization, in aurally oriented musical cultures, extreme conformity to a standard version of performance is evidently found, for example, among those cultures in which errors in performance are (or were) punished (such as the Indians of the North Pacific Coast of North America). Certain other cultures permit (explicitly or implicitly) greater freedom for the performer to depart from a model. Thus, in some African music, individuals singing in groups are encouraged to deviate from the melody, thus creating a type of polyphony. In the gamelan music of Java and Bali, some of the musicians improvise, i. e., play their own versions of the main melody, but with the use of certain traditionally used patterns, motifs and rhythmic types. In South Indian art music, the contribution of the performer to the total picture is still greater, but is limited by the establishment of specific types of improvisation, each with its rather precisely defined style characteristics: alapana, tanam, niraval, etc. In Arabic music, again, there is less typology of this sort, and the improvisor has only the barest of models: a scale and some characteristic motifs for each maqam, or mode and is perhaps closest to the almost completely unfettered improvisation of the western avant-garde improvisatory groups. Of course, many other intermediate examples could be cited. The point is that what is usually called improvisation is perhaps not really a phenomenon distinct from the performance of "composed" music. It revolves about one end of the continuum that exists between music in which the performer's role and contribution is small, and music in which it is overwhelmingly great. The evidence suggests that in some of the non- western cultures mentioned, the improvisor tends to see himself as a performer and interpreter of pre-existent music, rather than as a creator of the new.

In the performer-composer continuum, Persian music appears to be between Indian and Arabic. The name generally given to the improvised (and especially, but not exclusively, the non-metric) parts of Persian music is āvāz.

THE ĀVĀZ OF CHAHĀRGĀH, A REVIEW

IT MAY be useful to recapitulate here the main characteristics of āvāz in
Persian art music, [9] although this information is available also in various
fundamental publications on Persian music. Since the nineteenth century,
Persian music has been organized in a system of twelve dastgāhā, each of
which is characterized by a particular scale (i. e. a set of intervals as well
as a hierarchy of tones), to some extent a general musical character or
mood (although musicians neither stress this nor agree upon the specific
character of each dastgāh), and a number of parts, usually called gushehā
(literally, corners), which are performed in a more or less set order.
For example, in the case of chahārgāh, the scale, assuming C as the tonic,
is C, D-koron, E, F, G, A-koron, B, C. The suffix, koron, indicates a
note flatted slightly, less than a half-tone. According to some Iranian
theorists, it denotes flatting by a quarter-tone. In practice, there is a
great deal of variation in the intonation of the second and sixth degrees of the
chahārgāh scale, extending from something very close to a major second
or sixth, to a tempered minor second or sixth, from the tonic. The single
performance of chahārgāh recorded on the piano simply uses A-flat and D-flat.
Today, koron is symbolized by ⊅ in the notations used by some Persian musicians.

The most important parts or gushehā of chahārgāh, and their characteristics, are as follows: darāmad, which is sometimes simply called chahārgāh,
and is considered also the essence of chahārgāh, centering on the tonic; zābol
centering on the third; hesār, centering on the fifth, and in some versions
using tones that do not otherwise occur in the scale of chahārgāh and may
thus, according to Caron and Safvate, be called a modulation;[10] mokhālef,
centering on the sixth; muyyeh, which revolves about the fourth, and uses a
lowered fifth, thus constituting another modulation; maqlub, which uses mainly
the tetrachord from the fifth to the higher octave; and mansuri, whose center
is the higher octave of the tonic. These are the most important parts, and
while in some musicians' improvisations they possess characteristic tunes,
on the whole they are melodic skeletons with certain scalar characteristics and
certain very short motifs (sometimes with as few as two or three tones)
which characterize them.

In addition, there are parts of chahārgāh which are closer to being specific,
composed tunes, and whose performances are somewhat intermediate between
interpretation and improvisation. Among these are hodi, rajaz, and pahlavi,
all rather similar; and zanguleh, a tune which, because of its melodic range
and its contour, is usually considered a part of the darāmad. (There are
considerable differences of opinion among musicians regarding the terminology
of and theoretical relationships among these gushehā.) The parts of chahārgāh
mentioned here are the most frequently used; a few others are played
occasionally (but not always accepted as part of the canon of chahārgāh), for
example, rāk-e-abdollah, chahārbeyti, and yati maq.

These _gusheha_ may appear in a number of performance types. Some-times they are played or sung in non-metric fashion, occasionally they appear metrically in a manner known as _zarbi_ (drummed), perhaps with accompaniment of drum. Often the performance is a combination of metric and non-metric material, and of intermediate styles with varying degrees of metricity. In such combinations, performance in _zarbi_ style is often preceded and followed by non-metric material of the same _gusheh_. _Zarbi_ performances may be classed according to their meter (6/8, 3/4, 6/16, etc.). Also used are certain specific rhythm patterns, related to forms of poetry. A common one used in _chahārgāh_ as well as other _dastgāhā_ is _kereshmeh_, with the basic rhythm ♪♪♪♪♩♩. Vocal performances have much less metric material, except for solos by the instrumental accompanists, than do the purely instrumental performances.

An important part of any _dastgāh_ is the _forud_ (literally, descent), a fairly well established melodic pattern which can be used at the end of any _gusheh_ to lead the listener back to the tonal and motivic material of the _darāmad_ which is, after all, the most characteristic part of the _dastgāh_. It is almost always used at the end of a performance, and usually also after other _gushehā_, particularly those whose scale is considerably removed, or which have modulated, from the main scale of the _dastgāh_. It is followed by parts of the _darāmad_ or at least by its closing formula, whose repeated appearance helps to unify the performance. Normally a _forud_ is from twenty seconds to a minute in length, descends gradually, and at the end presents the opening and closing formula of the _darāmad_ which, in _chahārgāh_, can be reduced simply to an interval, moving from the sixth degree up to the tonic.

In order to show the roles of the various parts of a _dastgāh_ in an instrumental performance, here, as an example, is an outline of Performance Number 13, in the collection on which this study is based, a performance lasting about thirty-five minutes, played on the violin. The analysis was made by the performer himself. All metric sections are especially labelled:

> darāmad
> second darāmad (the same material, presented somewhat differently)
> repetition (approximately) of the first darāmad
> a short section of zābol, ending with the close of darāmad
> zābol, presented more fully
> 3/8 zarbi in zābol
> forud to darāmad of chahārgāh
> zābol (new material)
> forud to darāmad of chahārgāh
> muyyeh
> forud to darāmad of chahārgāh
> hesār
> 3/4 zarbi in hesār (referred to by performer as waltz)
> 6/16 zarbi in hesār
> 6/8 chahār mezrāb in hesār (a virtuoso section, not improvised in
>   this case but composed by the performer's teacher)

15

forud to darāmad of chahārgāh
mokhālef
chahār mezrāb in mokhālef
forud to darāmad of chahārgāh
zanguleh (this could have been considered a recapitulation of daramad)
mansuri
zarbi in mansuri
forud (very short)
darāmad (brief return)
chahār mezrāb using the material of the darāmad

Another performance (Number 5) lasting only thirteen minutes, played on the <u>setar</u> had the following parts, according to the performer:

darāmad group { darāmad (in three distinct parts)
kereshmeh (rhythmic section based on darāmad material)
zanguleh and cadence of darāmad

zābol
tasnif (song, performed instrumentally, composed, based on zābol)
hesār
chahār mezrāb in hesār
mokhālef
forud to darāmad of chahārgāh

Both of the analyses were made by the performers after listening to the tapes they had made. From these outlines it can again be seen that the section and material known as <u>darāmad</u> is the most fundamental and characterizing of the <u>dastgāh</u>. However before considering in detail some of the ways in which the <u>darāmad</u> is performed, it must be pointed out that the concept of <u>darāmad</u> has further ramifications. As the main <u>gusheh</u> of a <u>dastgāh</u>, the concept is not widely used except among musicians of Tehran who studied with masters of the Mirza Abdollah and Darvish Khan schools. [11] On the other hand, it is important to know that each of the major <u>gushehā</u> itself may have a short section called by some musicians its <u>darāmad</u>, which serves to introduce that <u>gusheh</u> and characterize it most explicitly. Among musicians of Khorasan (and perhaps other areas removed from the Tehran tradition), this modern and rather tightly organized concept of <u>dastgāh</u> is not so developed. For example, the term <u>chahārgāh</u> may itself be used to denote simply the <u>darāmad</u> of <u>chahārgāh</u>, which is, then, often performed by itself and not linked to other <u>gushehā</u>; on the other hand, other <u>gusheha</u> such as <u>zābol</u>, <u>mansuri</u>, <u>mokhālef</u>, and <u>hesār</u> appear outside Tehran to have something of an independent existence and to be considered separable units that may be performed alone. Finally, the term <u>darāmad</u> is used in yet another way, indicating a manner of performing a <u>gusheh</u>. Thus, a teacher may play a <u>gusheh</u> three times in different ways, and say that he has given "three <u>darāmads</u> of that gusheh." As in many cultures, in Persia the fundamental terms such as <u>āvāz</u>, <u>gusheh</u>, and <u>darāmad</u> are among the most difficult to define simply. They are used in a number of ways, and in that respect, they are analogous to such elusive concepts in western terminology as tone and rhythm.

16

APPROACHES TO ANALYSIS

ACCORDING TO most musicians as well as the literature, a performance of Persian classical music is usually designated as a rendition of one dastgāh. When a musician says that he is performing, for instance, dastgāh-e-segāh, he may mean that the entire dastgāh is played, i.e. all (or at least, many) of the gushehā; or, instead, he may mean that only a few gushehā are included; or he may refer to the darāmad alone. A performance including several gushehā may be easily divisible into sections, one section for each gusheh; or the performer may move imperceptibly from one gusheh to another, without indicating the change by a pause, or even by using a forud or the closing formula of the darāmad at the end of a gusheh. Within a gusheh, he may refer briefly to other gushehā. At the end of a gusheh, he may present material from the darāmad for as much as a minute or two. Thus, the role of the concept of gusheh varies with performance and performer. When a recording is played for a musician for analysis, he frequently has difficulty in stating precisely what gusheh is being played at a particular moment, partly because of differences in terminology, but, more important, because the concept of gusheh indicates both broad sections of a performance and short motifs which may be inserted into other gushehā.

Furthermore, on the basis of discussions with musicians, of lessons, and of analysis, it would appear that there is much variety of opinion regarding just what constitutes a gusheh or a section of a dastgāh. Some musicians insist that the term gusheh denotes the entire, authoritative version, published or learned in oral tradition. For example, the concept of zābol, one of the most important gushehā in chahārgāh, can be considered equivalent to four or five pages of specific printed music, or three or four minutes of precisely learned music. Deviations from this may be called by informants "one musician's way of playing zābol," but the published or taught version is zābol "itself." Another way of identifying the concept of zābol is to say that it is anything revolving about the third degree of the scale of chahārgāh. A further way of defining the concept is to consider the heart of zābol as being a short motif, that which is normally used to begin a performance of zābol: .[12] If this approach is used, the Persian analyst will usually say that the short motif "is" zābol, and that what follows is merely "āvāz," or, in somewhat different words, "he is just playing now."

These differing conceptions of the idea of gusheh make analysis based solely on Persian analytical techniques difficult. If a performer announces that he is playing, say, the darāmad of chahārgāh, there is likely to be no difficulty in finding agreement that he is in fact doing so at the beginning, at which point a familiar motif, using tonic, lower sixth, and lower fifth is prominent, e.g. . As he continues, however, he is likely to use portions of the scale and even motifs which could lead the analyst to

17

feel that he has departed from darāmad. The performer, if asked to comment, may maintain that this makes no difference, that this is still darāmad, or he may admit that he is playing a "reminder" (eshareh) of another gusheh. In describing a performance of a part of a dastgāh other than darāmad, he may divide a gusheh into its own darāmad and additional material of a more generalized sort, the latter containing, perhaps, references to other gushehā.

Thus we find a typical performance divisible in at least three ways. We can divide it simply into large sections, each of them normally labeled with the name of gusheh. Another way would be to make a chart of characteristics of such gushehā and plot the distribution of these characteristics, and perhaps find that the broad sections overlap greatly in the use of each others' material. Thus, performances of darāmad often contain allusions to zābol (assuming for the moment that zābol is anything that revolves about the third degree). To give a concrete example, near the end of darāmad in Performance Number 11, there is a clear reference to hesār, including the usual raising of the fourth degree. More typically, most gushehā contain references to the darāmad, particularly the use of the main beginning and closing motif, and especially at the endings.

A third way of dividing a performance is into two types of material, thematic and episodic. The thematic material comprises the motifs which recur in many performances, which appear as the characteristic parts of teaching versions, which are often called "darāmad" by those musicians who divide a gusheh performance into this plus "āvāz, " and which are used in lessons and conversations to characterize or identify a gusheh. For example, would be a part of the thematic material of zābol; of hesār; and of darāmad itself. It is not difficult to separate these most typical motifs from material which is obviously non-thematic. But there is also a great deal of intermediate material, material that is an extension of the theme and based on it.

The analytical technique used in this paper is the division of a performance into relatively large sections, each considered one gusheh, or dominated by it. Normally the first large section is the darāmad. But having divided a performance into several large sections and isolated one which we here simply call darāmad, we must point out that this introductory section does not always constitute a single unit in the analyses provided by musicians themselves. In a number of cases, such a section was said by its performer to consist of several darāmadhā (e. g. first darāmad, second darāmad, repetition of the first darāmad), or of metric materials with special names (e. g. zanguleh, kereshmeh) that are normally associated with the darāmad. Thus, in the detailed breakdowns of two performances given above, the first three parts of each would be considered the whole darāmad in our analyses. The subdivisions, of course, also conveniently play a role in our analyses and are here referred to as "units. "

18

THE TEACHING OF IMPROVISATION

IN A study of Persian improvisation one of the most revealing things is an understanding of the way Persian music is taught to performers. Evidently there have been changes in the method of teaching, and a number of different approaches have been described. According to Khatchi,[13] one method is for the teacher to give each of a group of pupils a particular bit of music to memorize (by playing it without the use of written music), and then to require them to teach these sections to each other. Such a procedure would provide ample opportunity for developing the variety that is necessary for the kind of individually varied performance practice found in Persian music. According to Nour-Ali Borumand, this practice, although used in his youth, about 1920, was not respected because it provided little direct personal attention for students on the part of the teacher. According to him, private lessons were more the rule in the early twentieth century. Another method is for a teacher to instruct a group of students simultaneously, giving them, at each lesson, a certain amount of material to memorize. In both cases, the material to be memorized is the _radif_ "of the teacher, " that is, of a specific version of the _gushehā_ of each _dastgāh_. In the teaching methods described, the technique of improvisation is not taught directly. Each master develops a version of his own which he teaches with great precision to students, and they are expected to learn it exactly, as if it were a set composition. The fact that the _radifhā_ of various teachers differ somewhat is due in part to the fact that each musician, once he has learned his master's _radif_, may set out to create his own version, making changes and innovations, and also in part because many musicians studied, successively or simultaneously, with two or more teachers and created their own _radifhā_ by combining their teachers' versions. Nevertheless, except for differences in terminology, several of the teaching versions used in Tehran in 1969 (evidently, in contrast to some of those used in other parts of the country) do not differ very significantly from each other.

The use of printed versions of the _radif_ is today widespread, and there are at least four different versions of parts of the radif in use by conservatories and private teachers. [14] Their use does not differ significantly from that of the orally-transmitted _radifhā_; the student learns them precisely by heart and does not perform from printed notes.

The amount of help given by teachers in the learning of improvisation appears to be small. In some cases teachers will play ornamented and otherwise varied versions of sections of the music for their students, and the students repeat these as a way of learning improvisation; but this method does not seem to be common. Two points mitigate this lack of teaching: 1) the fact that the teachers' versions of the _radif_ do not differ structurally from improvised versions is in itself an aid to learning improvisation. The difference between the model and the improvisation is one of detail, not essence.

If, for example, there were only a scale taught to the student and he were asked to improvise on this, his task would be very different and probably difficult. But the teacher says, in effect, "play something similar to what I'm playing," not, "improvise something on this model." Thus the student has the opportunity of departing very gradually from the teaching version, at first perhaps doing little beyond adding ornaments, repetitions, and brief extentions, later striking out more on his own. As will be seen later, performers devise melodic turns and formulae characteristic of their own improvisation but not found in teaching versions, and the degree of adherence to the teaching version differs with the performer. 2) For any gusheh, a master may teach several versions. For example, one master regularly teaches four different versions of the darāmad of chahārgāh to his students. They are similar, especially at their beginnings and endings, but also differ considerably in detail. Each student learns all four versions. It seems likely that this is one way in which a teacher can transmit the concept of individual variation or improvisation while retaining also the idea of adherence to stylistic orthodoxy. The performer must walk the narrow line between keeping the classical tradition intact -- it is easy to be criticized for departure from this tradition -- and establishing his personality as a performer through his own style of improvisation, and maintaining the flexibility which makes it possible for him to create innovations in each performance.

One of the interesting points to be noted is the number of persons, especially in Khorasan, who claimed to have learned the radif without a teacher, usually from printed versions. Their performances were usually shorter and less impressive than those of more formally schooled musicians, but one cannot maintain that they differ, as a group, from the others in the techniques of improvisation and the details of performance practice.

According to Zonis, [15] improvisation in Persian music depends on a number of decisions -- what gushehā to play, in what order, and in what fashion to perform each one. The most important aspect of these decisions would appear to be the last, since this provides the greatest opportunity for variation among performers and performances. The most important task of this paper is examination of this aspect of performance practice with the use of only one section of the radif of chahārgāh, the darāmad. The first two of Zonis' levels of musical decision-making, however, also are of interest here but they require the examination of entire performances of chahārgāh rather than just the darāmad.

One final point to be noted in a discussion of the relationship of learning to performance is the distinction made by Caron and Safvate[16] between two levels of improvisation, great and small. According to these authors, "great" improvisation involves decisions regarding the selection and order of gushehā; "small" improvisation involves such matters as ornamentation. Since one of the authors is himself a distinguished Persian musician, this statement may

20

genuinely reflect the feelings of the musicians. The intermediate areas between these two extreme levels, which is the material with which we are mainly concerned here, may, thus, be considered least subject to individual or performance variation. Possibly, then, these intermediate areas, thematic content, over-all structure, relationship of sections to each other within a gusheh, which provide the vehicles for a broad range of performance types, are part of what is learned from a teacher or developed in somewhat standardized form by an accomplished musician. Perhaps -- if we may anticipate a conclusion -- there is less variation within a musician's corpus of performances in the intermediate areas, and we may have to consider them part of what is learned by each performer and what becomes his model, rather than the main improvised materials. Such a conclusion would not detract from the importance of individual variation as a primary value in Persian classical music, but it would strengthen the feeling that what we are concerned with here is more performance practice than improvisation.

THE PERFORMANCES

THIS STUDY is based on forty-three performances of chahārgāh. The majority are by well-known professional musicians of Tehran and the north-eastern part of Iran, Khorasan, and a few come from commercial recordings or from publications. [17] There is a wide range of intensiveness and extensiveness of performance. Nevertheless, the performances can be classified in accordance with both musical and cultural criteria. Table I describes the recordings briefly and indicates the type of performance of each; in order to avoid embarrassment due to critical statements, performers are referred to by number, not by name.

Of considerable interest are the teaching versions, collected from three highly respected musicians, Performances Numbers 1, 2, and 19. These occupy a special place in our considerations, since they must be regarded both as models and as examples of performance. A number of performances were recorded especially for the investigator, i.e., elicited from musicians. Since a great deal of the final product of a performance depends on the performer, his mood, and his interaction with an audience, one may wish to question the validity of such recordings. It is certainly quite possible that a different range of performance times and total structure as well as of improvisatory detail may be found in performances made in studios or offices in the morning, at the request of a musicologist, than would be present in performances given in the relaxes atmosphere of men's social gatherings or garden parties, the most traditional milieu for classical music. Performances on such occasions are called majlesi, after the majles, colloquially perhaps translated as "sitting-around session. " The name applies to parties with music, food, drink, and occasionally opium, attended by perhaps four to eight

21

men. In the performances especially elicited, the musicians were asked to perform in the majlesi style. To what extent they were able to do so in detail can hardly be ascertained; but comparison on the basis of observation indicates that the differences are probably small. On the other hand, attempts to record actual performances at social gatherings turned out to cause such changes in the attitudes of those present that such recordings would almost certainly be as unreliable as the elicited recordings. The majlesi performances collected extend in length from ten to forty minutes and, as a group, exhibit the largest degree of variety among the types of performances collected.

Another type of performance collected is perhaps in some ways inter-mediate between majlesi performances and teaching versions. These were elicited especially for this study and were specifically designated by the performers as improvised, but the performers evidently tried to show what they considered the most academic sort of improvisation, separating the gushehā by pauses and announcements. While these performances tend to have less value as samples of actual performance practice than do the majlesi performances, they help to illuminate the difference between model and finished performance because they tend to be particularly close to teaching versions.

A few performances took place in situations of public entertainment, such as concerts, theater and weddings. Often these were ensemble performances, in contrast to those described above, and besides the "improvised" āvāz section, they included metric, composed pieces such as pishdarāmadhā, as well as drumming. The improvisatory aspect of these performances seems, on the whole, to be less elaborate and interesting than in the majlesi performances.

Finally, several performances were recorded at radio and television studios. Such performances today constitute one of the major outlets for traditional Persian music. They vary from short, solo renditions indistin-guishable except in length from the majlesi type to traditional ensemble performances, usually vocal (in contrast to the typically instrumental majlesi), and to ensemble performances that use orchestras of traditional and western instruments for the metric sections. Some performances were little more than short bits of āvāz surrounded by longer, westernized metric songs, and some consisted of music used as background for poetry recitation. It is in the area of radio performances that one finds some of the best examples of traditional improvisation, but, perhaps more interesting, one also finds reflected in them many different manifestations of culture change.

In summary, although a considerable proportion of the recordings on which this study is based was especially solicited, they can probably be considered a rather reliable sample of the types of performances found in Persian traditional music today.

THE ROLE OF DARĀMAD IN CHAHĀRGĀH PERFORMANCES

ONE APPROACH to understanding the performers practice of darāmad of chahārgāh is to examine its role, position, and distribution in the performances and its relationship in these respects to the other gushehā. Although clearly the most important single part of chahārgāh in both quantitative and qualitative sense, the darāmad occupies in these respects a position analogous to the other gushehā. The analyses of the thirty-six performances given in Table II are based on division of each performance into large sections, each labelled by the name of the gusheh which dominates it, and, as indicated in the section, "Approaches to Analysis, " not taking into account momentary departures and brief references to other gushehā.

In spite of the variety of performances, a clear pattern is evident. Darāmad appears in thirty-three of the performances as a separate, identifiable section. Of course, if closer analysis were made it would also appear in the other three because its main motif appears at the cadential points in other gushehā. As expected, it is the most important unifying factor in a performance of chahārgāh. Of the thirty-three performances in which it appears, it is the first part of the āvāz in thirty-one. Two performances begin with other gushehā, but present the darāmad in second or third place, giving it the role of a sort of a dramatic climax.

Zābol, built on the third degree of the scale, is also found in thirty-three of the performances and forms an almost inseparable unit with the darāmad, the two making up a sort of minimum subject matter for a performance of chahārgāh. It appears second in all but five of these performances, comes at the beginning in three, and is near the beginning in the remaining two.

Among the gushehā which appear most frequently, mokhālef (revolving between third and sixth) and hesār (revolving about the fifth, usually with a raised fourth) occupy a mediant position in most of the performances. Mokhālef appears to be the more important, appearing in twenty-seven performances, while hesār appears in sixteen. Mokhālef appears as the third gusheh in thirteen performances, the fourth in nine, the fifth in three, the first in one, and the second in one. It is interesting to find that the three most frequently used parts of chahārgāh are also the only ones (with the exception of hodi, in Performance Number 14, purposely played in an unusual manner by the performer) that are used to begin a performance.

Hesār appears as the third gusheh in seven performances, the fourth in five, the sixth in two, the second and the fifth once each. Hesār and mokhālef appear together in fourteen performances, and in all but one of these they are neighbors. Their order can evidently vary. The teaching versions indicate that hesār should precede mokhālef, but the other eleven performances show mokhālef preceding five times, and hesār, six times. This sort of inter-changeability between a pair of gushehā does not seem to be found among any other pairs or groups in chahārgāh.

Three other gushehā also were frequently used. Mansuri, revolving about the upper octave of the tonic, is found in twelve; in each case it is the final gusheh. Two others are used with some frequency: maqlub, using the tetrachord between fifth and octave, is found in seven performances. In six of these its position is after mokhālef or hesār. Muyyeh, revolving about the pentachord from tonic to fifth, frequently with a flatted fifth, is found nine times, six of these following zābol and preceding hesār or mokhālef.

The other gushehā used in the thirty-six performances analyzed are definitely rare. Hodi is used three times, but two of these are in teaching versions, in which it appears near the end; the other occurrence is at the beginning of an unusual performance in which darāmad does not appear at all. Rajaz, a song-like melody, similarly appears only in the two teaching versions and once elsewhere. Pahlavi and Bastenegar appear only in teaching versions. Hozān, yati maq, Rāk-e-Abdollah, and Chahārbeyti appear once each in non-teaching performances but did not appear in the recorded teaching versions, although some of them are found in some of the published teaching versions.

We may conclude that the various parts of chahārgāh can be classed in three groups: darāmad, zābol, and mokhālef seem to be the heart of this dastgāh, appearing in by far the majority of performances. Hesār, mansuri, maqlub and muyyeh are moderately common, tending to appear in the more extensive performances. The others are rare and were used primarily in teaching versions, in which attempts at completeness were made by the masters who provided them, or in performances which the musicians consciously tried to make unusual.

The role of darāmad in the performances of chahārgāh can be seen in its frequency and position, as well as in its relative length in the performances. Table II gives the information provided in the paragraphs above in somewhat more extensive form, indicating the specific inclusion and order of the gushehā in all of the performances, and indicating also the length of the darāmad (in seconds) compared to the total length of the performance. The picture that emerges is one of great variety. Performances of the darāmad vary from thirty seconds to six minutes, and from occupying the major portion of the entire dastgāh (e. g. Performance Number 5) to being one of a number of more or less equally important gushehā (e. g. Performances Numbers 6, 15, etc.).

THE UNIFIED treatment of the darāmad as well as the variety found in the assessment of its structural position and distribution is also found in the use of thematic material.

An examination of the performances indicates that a number of separate and, on the whole, distinct themes or motifs are used. In addition to centering about the tonic of the mode and of having a characteristic melodic interval that appears initially, cadentially, and at various medial points, the darāmad can be defined by a group of these themes, one or several of which appear in most performances, though not in all. The recordings made in Khorasan, particularly, tend to use few of these themes and present more variety of arrangements of order.

Table III gives these themes. As might be expected, rigid adherence to a single norm for each theme is not practiced. Instead, each performer provides variants and variations. The particular versions of the themes used for the table were taken from teaching versions of performers 1, 2, and 19. The order in which they appear in the table is of no significance. Usually the beginning of a "theme" is its most characteristic portion, while the last part is often varied, breaks into a sequence, or moves imperceptibly into another theme or an episode.

Table VI gives the distribution of these themes in the performances of the darāmad of chahārgāh indicated in Table II, as well as in one additional teaching version (1b), one improvisation on the darāmad (19a), and in four of the published radifhā (Numbers 37-40). The Arabic numerals in the left-hand column of Table VI indicate performance numbers (darāmad numbers) as in Tables I and II. The Roman numerals in the top row are the theme numbers as given in Table III. The main portion of the table indicates the distribution of the themes, the numbers giving the order in which they appear. For example, in Performance Number 1a, the order of appearance of the themes is I, VI, VIII, I etc. The horizontal divisions within some of the performances separate sections of the largest order, or units. If such a division extends into the "comments" column, this indicates that the sectioning and designations were given by the performer himself. The ordinal numbers in these units start afresh because each such unit could be considered as a separate performance of a darāmad as was the case, for example, in Performance Number 1a, whose performer clearly labeled the sections as indicated. However, in the analysis given here, they are considered as subsidiary units rather than separate darāmads. The number of daramads and units of each type of performance is given in Table IV; it must be remembered that while the total number of performances of chahārgāh listed in Table VI is forty-three, only forty actually have a daramad.

Each daramad analyzed in terms of these themes made use of at least three, and the characteristic number of themes used in a performance was four to six; the maximum was nine. A theme may appear more than once in the course of the performance of a darāmad. There is some direct correlation among the length of a darāmad, the number of units it has, and the number of themes it uses.

It is also clear that certain themes are much more widely used than others. Theme I, which is an elaboration of the main interval-motif of chahārgāh, is, of course, by far the most widely used. Themes VIII, VI, III, VII, and XI, given here in order of their frequency, also appear to be very popular. The other themes are used less frequently or even rarely. Most of these but especially Themes IV, V, and IX, are metric in character, as opposed to the more common themes which are performed non-metrically or in intermediate fashion. Theme XII seems to be peculiar to Performance Number 19, and is similar to Theme VII.

The more common themes can be separated into two groups on the basis of several criteria: Themes I, VIII, and VI in one group and Themes III, VII, and XI in the other. Those in the first group are characterized by their relatively greater frequency, although, at least in performances other than teaching versions, themes of the second group are slightly more common than Theme VI. In teaching versions, the first group is far more frequent than the second. Themes in the first group seem to have certain definite positions and functions within the darāmad. Theme I is used as an opening and closing motif in a darāmad or in a unit; Theme VI is usually the first motif after the opening Theme I; Theme VIII is used as a cadential motif preceding the final appearance of Theme I, or sometimes as a closing motif. Themes in a second group are used mostly in intermediate positions. The themes of the first group are within the characteristic melodic range of the darāmad of chahārgāh, i.e., from the fourth below the tonic to the third above, although Theme VI is at times extended to the sixth above the tonic. The themes in the second group are all above the tonic, consequently not including the most characteristic part of the mode of chahārgāh as indicated by Theme I. Finally, themes in the first group are the more stable, almost always occurring in the form given in Table III. This is especially true of Themes I and VIII, because they are used cadentially. Theme VI shows somewhat more variation, perhaps because it leads into the more characteristically improvisatory part of a darāmad or unit subdivision, namely, into the center portion. The themes of the second group are varied considerably, presenting a continuum from forms more or less precisely as given in Table III to others which are merely vague hints of the thematic characteristics. At times, only the general range and tonal material of the theme are indicated; this is often the case with Theme VII, with its emphasis on the third degree of the mode. A general downward movement from the upper octave to the tonic is a feature of Theme XI. The identification of Themes VII and XI is further complicated by the fact that they vaguely resemble, in structure and function, respectively, the gusheh zābol and the forud to chahārgāh (i. e. the descent to the cadential formula). Some variations of Theme VII, for instance, would be called 'eshare-ye' zābol ("reminder" of zābol) by some performers (e.g. Performance Number 9).

Since Themes I, VIII, and VI seem to be, in terms of frequency and standardization, most characteristic of the darāmad of chahārgāh, it seems appropriate to make a special examination of their use in the forty darāmad performances. We will distinguish among the categories of performances: teaching versions, solo performances recorded in Tehran, ensemble performances recorded in Tehran, and performances from Khorasan. In Table V, the distribution of themes in the darāmadhā of these performance categories is given.

In all four categories of performance, the order of frequency of themes in Group I is I, VIII, and VI. They are present in all of the teaching versions, but not in all of the other performances. Theme I is present in all but one performance, the exception being from Khorasan. It is the beginning of all darāmad performances except of three from Khorasan. Thirty of forty darāmadhā also end on this theme, the exceptions being one teaching version, seven solo performances, and two from Khorasan. Two-thirds of all darāmadhā both open and close with this motif. Proportionally, most of the exceptions are from Khorasan. Eighty-four out of eighty-nine daramad units (see p18 for definition of this term) contain Theme I. Most units in all categories start and/ or end with this theme. Exceptions are most common in the performances from Khorasan. Even where Theme I is not present in the form given in Table III, the basic interval of this theme, i.e. A♭ to C, is usually present at beginnings and endings. Thus, characteristically, Theme I is used for opening or closing (slightly less common), or both, but this is more characteristic of teaching version performances and least of those from Khorasan.

Theme VIII is present in thirty-two of the forty darāmad performances and in all of the teaching versions. The eight exceptions are proportionally divided among the solo, ensemble, and Khorasan categories. In more than four-fifths of the performances and in all of those in the ensemble category, it appears either in the penultimate position in a unit followed by Theme I, or, much less characteristically, it is used to end the unit. Again, most of the exceptions are found in the Khorasan performances. Whenever it occurs near the end of a darāmad it is followed only by Theme I. Occasionally a darāmad may end on Theme VIII.

Theme VI is present in slightly more than half of the darāmad performances and in all of the teaching versions. It is not present in any of the eight performances from Khorasan. In twenty-eight out of the thirty appearances it is preceded by Theme I, by which it is also followed in slightly more than half. It is absent in two-thirds of the performance units and is most characteristically present in beginning units.

Themes I, VIII, and VI are all present, together, in half of the darāmadhā and in all of the teaching versions, but in none of the Khorasan versions. One-fourth of all of the performances and three-fourths of the teaching versions are built essentially within the thematic framework:

$$I \longrightarrow VI \quad \cdots\cdots\cdots \quad VIII \longrightarrow I$$

The characteristics of distribution of Themes I, VIII, and VI, appear most frequently in the performances by musicians associated with the Conservatory of National Music in Tehran, and less so in those of musicians not belonging to any of the schools or living in Khorasan.

The preceding analysis of thematic materials again provides only one of several possible avenues of approach to an understanding of the performances of the darāmad of chahārgāh. What has been discussed is essentially the more stable elements, while those which serve best to distinguish performances and performers have only been touched upon. The following section presents individual analysis of nine performances, stressing differences in structure, tempo, dynamics, phraseology, and other elements of performance practice as well as the treatment of themes.

NINE SELECTED PERFORMANCES

IN THE preceding section it was shown that a group of themes act as a common denominator among performances of chahārgāh, and that performers not only make selections from these themes but also tend to use them in a particular order and at specific points in a performance. The performances most alike in this respect were those from Tehran, especially that those were associated with the Conservatory of National Music. In order to provide somewhat more detailed description of the similarities and differences among the performances, we now turn to individual discussion of nine representative recordings.

Number 28. The darāmad of Performance Number 28 is preceded by an introductory section composed of a pishdarāmad, a non-metric moqadameh (introduction), and a chahār mezrāb. The first of its two major sections is characterized by rather slow tempo, moderate dynamic level, and, since it is a vocal rendition, by a somewhat deliberate type of delivery evidently conditioned by the rhythm of the poetry. It is accompanied by the violin in imitative and heterophonic style. Its first half is taken up by two variations of a statement of the main theme of chahārgāh, Theme I (see Table III), performed in a slow and pensive manner. This could be called the darāmad of the darāmad. Some momentum is gathered with the introduction of Themes VII and VIII and the climax of the section is reached on g'' during the sequential extension of Theme VIII only to subside again to c''. The second major

28

subdivision, although a variant of the first, is different from it in all other aspects. It is a hurried and condensed restatement of the melodic material of the first section by the violin alone, and it has somewhat of the character of an afterthought or summary.

This darāmad is rather close in structure and performance practice to the teaching versions. It uses the common technique of building intensity through achieving a melodic or pitch climax paralleled by a gradually increasing tempo and dynamics as well as by use of ornamentation and thematic development. The thematic material used is rather close to the models given in Table III. The comparatively limited range of an octave, the short duration, and the sparing use of sequence, extension and other developmental devices also suggest close relationship to the teaching versions.

Number 19a. Performance Number 19a was designated by its performer as an improvisation on the darāmad and it was played by him before 19b, which is the version he uses in teaching.

Although it is readily divisible into three long sections, we found it harder to discover smaller formal units in this performance than in most others. One of the unique features is its choppy phrasing, often separated by long rests that seem to prevent the development of a climax or of intensity. Otherwise, the phrases are varied somewhat in the fashion of Performance Number 3 with the added contrasts of range, and an effect created by the contrastive timbre of the lower register of the nai which is produced by a different technique of blowing. The first and third sections of this performance are in the āvāz style, the third one being similar to the last part of the much larger first section. The middle section is in the metric style and is characterized by repetitions of the rhythmic motif: ♪♪♪♪. Its contrastive character and its position just before the short closing āvāz gives it the role of climax of the whole darāmad. The āvāz sections follow the common practice of brief thematic developments separated by episodes and/or minor cadences. Thus, three Themes (XI, XII, and VII) are varied and developed in its Section A.

Number 16. Similarly to Number 28, the darāmad of Performance Number 16 follows a general introductory section, composed of a moqadameh, a pish-darāmad, and a chahār mezrāb, which contain features of the darāmad and of two gushehā, zābol and mokhālef, of chahārgāh. The darāmad proper includes two sections contrasting not only in the choice of thematic material, but also in the style of performance. Section 1 uses Themes I, II and VIII, with Theme II predominating; Section 2 uses primarily Theme III, but also Theme VIII. The metrically free first section is in contrast to the zarbi style used in the second section. More striking than these contrasts, however, are the similarities between the sections. Both use the same one-octave range and similar melodic contours (since Themes II and III are alike in this respect). As mentioned above, the core of each section is the development of one thematic idea. In both, the respective themes are stated twice, slightly varied, and a third time in an extended and elaborated form. The tempo is slow and about the same for both sections. In parallel fashion, both sections increase slightly in intensity during the development of the main themes through a melodic climax, a gradual accelerando, an increase in rhythmic vitality, and an increase in dynamic level. Despite the use of the contrasting āvāz and zarbi styles, however, this darāmad is characterized by its rather static nature on all levels of construction and performance. Perhaps this is partially due to the rather limited resources of the kamānge.

Darāmad Number 16 is similar to teaching versions in the same way as Performance Number 28 was shown to be.

Number 15. The two major sections of Performance Number 15 were designated by the performer as "first" and "second" darāmad; each of these has two subsections of unequal length. With the exception of the second subsection in A, all occupy the upper octave and descend to the lower one towards the end. The second section of A is entirely in the lower octave. The climax in Section A is reached on e" and is closer to the beginning than usual. The second half of this section is interesting because it is a special form of the improvisation technique already mentioned with regard to Performances Numbers 6 and 16, but in this case the starting motif of Theme I and its repetitions are slowly transformed into Theme VIII, by the final expanded variation. Section B begins with the kereshmeh rhythm (𝄢 𝄢 𝄢) but it changes to the āvāz style after the first two phrases. The thematic material is fairly close to that of teaching versions.

Number 6. Performance Number 6 consists of three progressively longer sections, the first two of which are variants of each other. The third section contrasts with these two not only in the use of different thematic material, but also in the manner of performance. It moves more quickly and is more contrastive in its phrasing, somewhat resembling Performance Number 3. It differs from the first two sections in that it achieves energy through thematic development and an insistent drive downward, whereas the first two reach climaxes at the peaks of arc-shaped contours. This is the result of the particular themes used in the sections: Theme VI in Sections 1 and 2, and Themes X and VIII and their variants in Section 3. It is interesting to find that the climaxes of the first two sections on e" are reflected by the climax of Section 3, and of the entire darāmad, a strong downward movement to e. The three sections move progressively away from the most widely used "teaching version." The first is an almost precise rendition of this version; the second, a variant of it, largely an octave higher; and the third, an improvised extension using new material, back in the lower octave. The last section contains some excellent examples of thematic development of the type found in Persian classical music. Each of the three themes, or fragments thereof, used in this section are repeated one to three times followed by a much elaborated, varied, and extended final rendition each faster and louder than the previous one.

30

Number 33. Performance Number 33 from Khorasan exhibits a simple A^1A^2 form, in which the second section is an extended variation of the general melodic material of the first. Both subdivisions are descending in contour through the range c" - c', with the second section dropping down another octave for its last few phrases and ending on c. As might be expected, on the basis of some of the discussion above, the themes of the darāmad, with the exception of Theme I, resemble those of the teaching versions only in very superficial ways, such as their general melodic direction and range. Furthermore, the difference of this performance from those recorded in Tehran is accentuated by the already mentioned predominance of descending contours, the similarity of the only two sections, and the rather even and uneventful mode of delivery. It does not give the listener a sense of climax or of building up of intensity.

Number 5. Darāmad Number 5, one of the longest performances, consists of five parts. Three of these belong to the daramad proper, one was designated by the performer as "kereshmeh, " and the last one, "zangouleh. " All of the darāmad sections are rather close, in structure and thematic material, to the teaching versions. The first of these is actually performed in the chahār mezrāb style. The other two present variations of a few themes in a very straightforward manner. The most interesting parts of this darāmad are the metric sections and especially the kereshmeh, in which the performance reaches its climax, specifically with the appearance of persistent syncopation found in the second half of the section, material somewhat reminiscent of the rhythmic agitation often found in the final portions of the gat in classical Indian music.

Number 12. Performance Number 12 is about the length of Number 5 and consists of four sections each of which is longer than the preceding one, and further removed in content from any of the teaching versions. Thus, Section D contains a long passage which does not seem to use any themes from teaching versions at all. This is one of the most quickly paced and highly ornamented among the performances here examined.

Number 3. In sharp contrast to Performance Number 33, which it resembles in certain structural features such as A^1A^2 form and predominantly descending contour, Performance Number 3 is perhaps one of the most varied ones here examined. It is characterized by alternation of several contrastive features rather than by the commonly found type of construction which builds toward a single melodic climax. A different sort of climax is achieved through the increasing frequency of alternation of these features. Dramatic contrast of phrases comes about through frequent changes from metric to non-metric, loud to soft, fast to slow, ornamented to plain, drone to lack of drone, as well as through contrasting melodic contours. A typical section of this performance moves gradually from the non-metrical into the metrical, which ends on a decisive cadence. Intensity in this piece is achieved in several ways: 1) the insistent downward movement; 2) motivic repetitions

31

and sequences which become faster, louder, and more intense in tone and then subside; 3) motivic expansions, as in the motif a♭' - g' - f' - e' in Section A; 4) the contrasting phrasing mentioned above. Another unique feature of this performance is the extensive use of vibrato (achieved by shaking of the instrument) as an ornament.

Some of the techniques of improvisation in this performance are worthy of examination in detail. After the initial complete statement of Theme I, the first part of a variant of Theme XI is presented in the āvāz style. Then it is repeated in the zarbi style in the form of a sequence with the addition of a crescendo, drone, and an extension down to c' at the end of the phrase. A fragmentary statement in the āvāz style of Themes VIII and VI provide contrast. Then, still in the āvāz style, the above used variant of Theme XI is presented an octave lower and then a third lower than the original. This is followed by repetitions and variations of a four-note scalar motif moving down to the third in a quasi-zarbi style. The following quick, loud scalar passage over a drone of f contrasts with a zarbi phrase that varies the descending scalar contour of Theme XI in the form of interlocking thirds over a drone on low c. Section A is concluded by the cadencial Theme VIII. Section A' starts with only the second, and slightly less characteristic, part of Theme I, followed by variants of the corresponding phrases of Section A. Then a fast, ornamented and loud descending scalar passage in the area of Theme XI leads to the cadential Theme VIII, which is the same as in Section A. One can clearly see that this darāmad consists of melodic material derived from the descending passage of Theme XI interrupted by a rare undeveloped appearance of other themes such as VIII and VI and, of course, the opening Theme I, and the closing Theme VIII.

COMPARISONS AND CONCLUSIONS

INTRODUCTORY AND restricted as it is, this study provides certain insights into the nature of Persian improvisation. But in generalizing from our findings, the reader must take into account the possibility that what is true of one part of a mode may not be true of others, and that the most significant portion of a dastgāh, the darāmad, may undergo treatment quite different from other, less typical gushehā. In the case of chahārgāh, there are examples to support this view. Thus, those gushehā that are essentially fixed melodies -- for example hodi, pahlavi, and rajaz -- hardly deviate from the norm in the few performances available. Others, such as mokhālef, appear to be much less rigorously defined than darāmad, being characterized essentially by scalar traits rather than themes, whereas darāmad has in practically all of its performances a typical cadential motif. Again, it may be that the kinds of conclusions that can be drawn for the darāmad of chahārgāh apply to the darāmadhā of all dastgāhā, or to the concept of darāmad in Persian music at large. Yet, there is evidence that conclusions of at least a slightly different sort would be drawn, for example, in an examination of the darāmad of shur, which does not have as striking a motif that keeps recurring, or of segāh, which has a typical interval pattern that, unlike the chahārgāh motif, appears at points other than the cadence. Thus, this study should be followed by similar examinations of other conceptual units in the corpus of Persian classical music.

Perhaps the most striking characteristic of the entire group of performances of chahārgāh is its range. We find a tremendous variety of lengths, themes, procedures, types of development, and structure. Nevertheless, the amount of common material in almost all of the performances is so great that it is difficult to disagree with the attitude of Persian musicians to the effect that what is really happening is interpretation of pre-existing material rather than constant creation of "new" music.

The most characteristic method of development in melody is also a feature that unites most of the performances. It relies on repetition, sequential treatment, and expansion of motifs for its structural features. Typically, a motif may be repeated twice, perhaps at different pitch levels, then expanded, after which a section of the expanded form is subjected to treatment similar to that described for the first motif. This results in the characteristically wave-like intensity curve of the music, with its short stretches of intensification and its large number of minor climaxes, a feature that sharply distinguishes the Persian non-metric improvisation from the more grandly organized Indian alap, and which on the other hand demonstrates a relationship to the similar but somewhat more "choppy" characteristic style of the Arabic taqsim. The kind of development described here is characteristic of most of the performances of the darāmad of chahārgāh, but particularly of the longer instrumental ones. It appears to be characteristic of Persian music at large, and while it is most common in the non-metric portions, it may also be found in the metric ones.

A number of the performances of the darāmad of chahārgāh constitute a homogeneous group, in so far as the thematic material is concerned. These are most typically the performances of musicians who studied at the Conservatory of National Music, or who are associated with that institution, and are very frequently based on the material in the published radif of Ma'aroufi. The performances of older musicians and of those living outside Tehran tend to deviate substantially from that model (or are perhaps not really related to it at all).

In terms of structure and organization of the performance, those of older musicians (e. g. Numbers 16, 3, 8 and 19) also tend to deviate from the homogeneous cluster of performances represented by the "Conservatory" group, as exemplified by Numbers 6, 10, 12, and 15, mainly in that they exhibit much greater variety.

The performances on the whole cannot easily be classified but fall into a group of relatively uninterrupted continua. It is not easy to class them in readily identifiable groups (e. g. long-short, metric- non-metric). Each variable is distributed more or less equally in the continuum between complete absence and strong presence. Nevertheless, it is possible to present here a few types of performances of the darāmad of chahārgāh, in accordance with the clustering of several variables.

One type of performance consists essentially of a teaching version, which is presented in embellished form, and which may be extended, but is given almost throughout in non-metric fashion. It is illustrated by the instrumental Performances Numbers 6 and 15, some of the versions collected in Khorasan, and most of the vocal performances. On the whole, this type of performance is shortest and seems to be regarded by musicians as the least interesting.

A second type has several distinct sections, most of them non-metric but some zarbi. It often includes a section with the kereshmeh rhythm, and a performance of zanguleh. This performance type tends to be longer and is exemplified by the Performances Numbers 5, 12, and 13.

A third performance type consists of relatively indistinct sectioning and rapid alternation between metric and non-metric material. It departs, in its use of themes, from the standard teaching versions and introduces material from other gushehā. This performance type seems to be more characteristic of older performers, and may represent an older form of improvisation which preceded the introduction of greater standardization that seems to have come about through institutions and publications.

It must also be pointed out that the vocal versions, no matter under what circumstances they were recorded, are much more standardized than the instrumental ones. Probably the reason involves the underlaying of the text. Typically, a vocal darāmad begins with an arc-shaped, vocalized, melismatic statement of the main motif and its extension. The same musical ground is then covered, somewhat more elaborately, with use of a poem, and the darāmad ends with a longer, melismatic passage that departs more from teaching versions. Zarbi sections rarely appear. The instrumental versions exhibit much more variety, but a few of them (e. g. Number 6) follow essentially the structure of the vocal performances.

A few performances do not readily conform to this typology. For example, Number 8 is zarbi almost throughout; Number 11 is largely in slow, pishdarāmad style and heptuple meter; Number 29, from Khorasan, exhibits a style somehow intermediate between the drawn-out, non-metric manner and zarbi, exhibiting a good deal of rhythmic regularity without metric precision. Nevertheless, the majority of performances do conform roughly to the types set out above.

34

One of the important objectives of this study was to find out the degree to which individual performers varied their practices and their content from performance to performance. Material for such observations has been gathered for five performers (although not all of these performances are included in the forty-three analyzed here), not counting the teaching versions. In general, it appears that performers differ in the degree to which their performances vary among themselves. The performer of Numbers 12, 13, and 14, although including a variety of materials in his recordings, tended to use the same procedures, motifs, melismatic structures, cadences, and other details of improvisation. The performer of Numbers 6 and 7 exhibited very little variety although his recordings were made about four years apart. The performer of Numbers 16, 17, and 18 exhibited more variety but included a number of highly idiosyncratic sections and themes. The same is true of the nai player in Performance Number 19, who was heard but not recorded on other occasions. The performer of Numbers 5 and 11, on the other hand, provided highly contrasting performances of chahārgāh in recordings made several years apart. The performers of Numbers 3 and 8 were heard several times but recorded only once. Their performances vary greatly in length and over-all structure, but exhibit considerable uniformity in both thematic content and details of improvisation such as ornamentation, type of alternations between non-metric and metric materials, the use of sequences, and dynamics.

If one compares the groups of performances by an individual musician with the entire range of performances present in this collection, one cannot escape the conclusion that each musician develops not only his own style, but beyond that, almost his own special version of the darāmad of chahārgāh, which he performs with variations, in different lengths and with some flexibility of content, but which can readily be distinguished as his own. Some musicians exhibit a greater degree of variety than others, but even in the music of the most inventive of them the pre-existing material occupies a role of enormous importance. Some of this material belongs to the corpus of devices common to chahārgāh, and some to the musician's idiosyncratic canon.

Despite the considerable variety in performance, performance types, and the differences among performers, we may perhaps speak of a "typical" way of performing the darāmad of chahārgāh. It normally begins and ends with the main, distinctive motif, and in its course, it builds intensity. This is accomplished in a number of ways, not all of them necessarily present in any single performance. For example, a performance may increasingly depart from the norm, or from what is expected or known by the listener, such as a teaching version. Another technique is to decrease the frequency of appearance of the main motif in the course of the performance. The average pitch level may rise to a climax, shortly before the end of darāmad. The average amount of tone material used in a subsection may increase as the darāmad progresses; ornamentation increases, and, especially in vocal performances, so does the amount of melisma. The performance tends to become louder, and subdivisions such as phrases tend to increase in length. These characteristics

35

are found in performances of other gushehā and other dastgāhā, but they seem by no means to be universal in Persian performance practice.

Certainly there are also performers who are unable to achieve the kind of intensification of the material that is usual; and of course, occasionally there is a performer who wishes to give, so to speak, the opposite impression. But on the whole, the structure of a performance of the darāmad of chahārgāh seems to be determined in advance by the need to use various techniques to build intensity, framed by statements of the main motif.

While this study is essentially synchronic, it does provide some tentative information towards an understanding of Persian music history of the twentieth century. Certain conclusions can be reached on the basis of comparison betwee older and younger musicians, of recent performances with earlier recordings, and of rural and urban performances, as well as the tracing of obvious western characteristics of style and of musical thought.

In the course of the twentieth century, a certain amount of standardization seems to have taken place in Persian performances. This is indicated by the greater clustering of performances by younger musicians in terms of thematic content and development procedure and seems to be related to the introduction of radio and television, to the fact that musicians gradually congregated in Tehran, and to the development of the Conservatory for National Music and its groups of associated musicians, as well as to the use of printed versions of the radif. Since the older musicians tend to deviate more from a norm, or to exhibit more variety in performance style and thematic content, one might wish to assume that there is now less variety in the range of performances of a conceptual unit such as the darāmad of chahārgāh than was the case in the pas There is, however, also reason to believe that the variety of performance styl is now actually greater than in the past and that the attrition of improvisat techniques is being replaced by some of the variety-producing factors of western music that have been adopted, such as the greater number of instrumental techniques available on the violin (compared to the kamānge) and the various kinds of western ensemble performances in concerts and on the radio.

The length of Persian performances seems to have decreased in step with the increased tempo of modern life. While the typical performance in earlier times at men's social gatherings or garden parties, for instance, had no time limit placed upon it, the most common types of modern performances made for radio, television, recordings, and the concert stage, are limited by technical consideration or convention. The degree to which listeners feel they have time to relax enough to listen seems also to have decreased. Thus, it is almost certain that the typical performance of Persian music is today shorter than it was several decades ago.

There are a number of ways in which the specifically musical characteris of western music (especially the classical music of the nineteenth century) see to have influenced the course of history of Persian classical music. One of the most obvious is the willingness to perform chahārgāh on instruments that are capable of producing only half-tones and multiples of half-tones, such as the piano, the clarinet, and the accordion. While it is said that a piano should be especially tuned for each dastgāh, some performances of chahārgāh are performed with the second and sixth tones lowered by a quarter-tone. Some of the performances on the violin also tended to use the western intonation, or moved in that direction.

The use of western instruments such as the violin (now the most widely used instrument in Persian classical music), clarinet, flute, piano, organ, and the use of a revived gheichak (a relative of the Indian sarinda once used primarily in folk and tribal music in Eastern Iran) strung and tuned like a violin, must also be mentioned. The use of specifically western performance techniques on the violin, such as pronounced vibrato, something not found, incidentally, in the South Indian use of the western violin, is also an important recent development.

No systematic study of intonation in the performances has been made. It has already been observed, however, that the intonation of the second and sixth degrees of the scale exhibit the greatest variety extending, respectively, from minor second and sixth, above the tonic, to an interval almost the size of major second and sixth. This variety is, of course, most evident in performances on unfretted instruments, particularly the violin. Although one could advance various psychological and acoustical explanations of this phenomenon, the most plausible one seems to be the influence of western music and its tempered scale which does not include these intervals of chahārgāh. Iranian musicians accustomed to hearing western music may have become ambivalent about the intonation of the three-quarter tones. Among the recordings used here, there is some evidence that indicates that those musicians most exposed to western music intone the second and sixth degrees of the scale lower than do others. We should also point out that lowering these pitches is a deviation from the traditional model of the chahārgāh scale, but one that does not conflict with other Persian modes; raising them instead would also have approximated western intonation, but it would also have assimilated the chahārgāh scale to that of the dastgāh of Māhour.

The general character of the typical performances by younger musicians is distinguished by traits evidently derived from western music. Among them is the occasional use of chords and major-triad arpeggios, the marked beginnings of sections and the strong cadences, and a heroic style of annunciating the main motif. The relatively large amount of metrical material may also be the result of exposure to the constantly metric western music. The zarbi and chahār mezrāb sections are more prominent and are labeled in western metrical terms, such as 6/8 and 6/16, and sometimes even by the names of western genres such as "waltz."

37

Beyond these specific traits, however, the general mood of the typical performances by younger musicians differs from that of the older ones. The latter have a quiet, sometimes vague, and perhaps mystical character; the younger musicians usually appear more positive, more cognizant of an audience more precise in the articulation of themes, beginnings, and cadences. Althoug the content of their performances is certainly the radif of Persian classical music, the character of the music is much more inclined towards performance standards in nineteenth century western music. There are those who may lament the loss of some of the typical traits of Persian performance practice, but there is also no doubt that the acceptance of certain western elements in musical thought and practice have made it possible for the essence of Persian classical music to survive in a modern and increasingly western-oriented cultural environment.

1. It is interesting to find the large amount of attention that has been given to the theoretical system of Persian music, i. e. , the system of the dastgāhā, as it is articulated by living musicians, in contrast to the very small amount of attention given to the nature and structure of actual performances of music. One of the important tasks of musicology in the future is the development of a system of describing and comparing individual performances and individual performers of materials that is largely improvised.

2. Hormoz Farhat, The Dastgāh Concept in Persian Classical Music. Unpublished dissertation, UCLA, 1966.

3. Ella Zonis, "Contemporary Art Music in Persia, " Musical Quarterly 51 (1965) 636-48; see also her forthcoming general book on Persian music, to be published by Harvard University Press.

4. Nelly Caron and Dariouche Safvate, Iran, in the series, Les Traditions Musicales (Paris, 1966).

5. Edith Gerson-Kiwi, The Persian Doctrine of Dastgāh Composition (Tel-Aviv, 1963).

6. Khatschi Khatschi, Der Dastgāh (Regensburg, 1962).

7. Mohammed Massudieh, Āwāz-e-Šur (Regensburg, 1968).

8. Eckart Wilkens, Künstler und Amateure im persischen Santurspiel (Regensburg, 1967).

9. The word, āvāz, like important words pertaining to music in English such as "tone, " appears to have several meanings or a broad range of meaning. It refers to the non-metric improvised portions of classical music, it may refer to improvised music at large, it may refer specifically to vocal improvised music, vocal music at large, or it may have a meaning somewhat equivalent to "song. "

10. Caron and Safvate, op. cit., p. 83.

11. These important schools of musicians are discussed in detail by Khatschi, op. cit., pp. 1-52, and Zonis, op. cit., pp. 638-9.

12. The word koron, and the symbol ꞓ indicate a lowering of approximately a quarter-tone.

13. Khatschi, op. cit., pp. 33-5.

14. The authors of these four most important collections of material that function as teaching versions are Ali Naqi Vaziri, Abolhassan Sabā (probably the most widely used), Ruhollah Khāleqi, and Musa Ma'aroufi. The publications of the first three appear under various imprints and in a number of different forms of organization, and include methods for learning specific instruments as well as set compositions in addition to the parts of the radif. They were published by various small printing houses in Tehran, in varying arrangements of volumes and organization. Ma'aroufi's radif appears in Mehdi Barkechli, La musique traditionelle de l'Iran (Tehran, 1963), and is by far the most extensive of the four.

15. Zonis, op. cit., p. 641.

16. Caron and Safvate, op. cit., p. 129.

17. Ma'aroufi's radif, in Mehdi Barkechli, La musique traditionelle de L'Iran (Tehran, 1963).

TABLES

TABLE I

BRIEF SKETCHES OF THE MUSICIANS

TEACHING VERSIONS

1. Highly respected musician in his sixties, student of important masters
   of early twentieth century, including Darvish Khan and Musa Ma'arouffi.
   Performed on tār and setār. Performance 1B was recorded in 1967.
2. Respected musician in his forties, teacher at Conservatory of National
   Music, student of Musa Ma'arouffi and Abolhassan Saba. Singer

SOLO PERFORMANCES RECORDED IN TEHRAN

Setār:

3. Famous older musician, student of masters of early twentieth century.
   Important today as performer on radio and television.
4. Performance on commercial record, performer not named. The style
   indicates that it may be the performer of Number 3. Santur, Tunbuk,
   and Tār; music and drum rhythms from Iran. Limelight: LS-86057.
5. Well-known performer in his forties, student of the performer of Number
   1. Known as scholar and teacher; spent several years living in Europe.

Tār:

6. Young performer, teacher at Conservatory for National Music; student
   of Saba.
7. Same as Number 6, but commercially recorded. Classical music of
   Tren. Folkways: FW 8831, Volume 1.

Santour:

8. Famous performer in his forties, not associated with any school of
   musicians. Widely heard on radio and television, and on records; has
   toured in Europe and Asia.
9. Music of Iran; Santur Recital; Volume 2. Lyrichord: LL-165.
10. Young performer, teacher at Conservatory of National Music; student
    of Saba.
11. Same as Number 5.

Violin:

12. Young violinist who plays both western and Persian music; graduate of
    Conservatory of National Music; student of Habibollah Badi'i. Not well known.
13. Same as Number 12.
14. Same as Number 12.
15. Moderately known violinist in his forties; teacher at Conservatory of National
    Music; pupil of Saba.

Kamāngé:

16. Famous kamange player in his fifties; not associated with any school of musicians; teaches at University of Tehran; widely heard on television; has toured abroad.
17. Same as Number 16, recorded ca. a month later than Number 16.
18. Same as Number 16; taken from commercial recording made before Number 16. The Music of Iran, Volume 1 (Unesco Collection). Bärenreiter: 30 L2004.

Nai:

19. Famous nai player, not associated with any school of musicians; heard widely on radio and television.

Piano:

20. Young female pianist; teacher at Conservatory of National Music; pupil of performer of Number 2; performs western and Persian music.

ENSEMBLE PERFORMANCES RECORDED IN TEHRAN

21. Commercial recording of very popular female singer, accompanied by well-known tār player respected for his knowledge of classical tradition. Avāz-e Banu-e Delkash (Ahang IR LP 20002, B2)
22. Performance for radio, with two vocal soloists, a nai player (same as in Performance Number 19), small orchestra of Iranian and western instruments, and a speaker who recites poems. This is a modern performance, but the performers are individuals who are able to perform in a more traditional style as well.
23. Singer (same as performer of Tape Number 2) with a student accompanying him on the nai. The student is an amateur who otherwise studies architecture.
24. Violin, tār, and drum; performers are lower-class musicians who play for weddings and in music halls, and who know classical as well as local popular styles.
25. Radio performance, with a well-known female singer, a highly-respected santour player (who is distinguished for his knowledge of classical tradition) and a drummer, with orchestral prelude.
26. Concert performance, with two well-known singers and a famous violinist, orchestra, and a speaker who recites poems.
27. Concert performance, with one of the two or three most popular singers of Iran (who more frequently sings popular music), a well-known violinist, a moderately known santour player, a drummer, orchestra, and a speaker.
28. Majlesi-style performance, with a famous singer, ca. sixty years old, a moderately known violinist, and an amateur drummer. All musicians are originally from Tehran, but recording was made in Tel-Aviv.

PERFORMANCES RECORDED IN KHORASAN

Tār:

29. Part-time musician, ca. sixty years old, otherwise watch repairman.
    First language Turkish. Lives in Bojnurd.
30. Musician ca. thirty, pupil of Number 29. Performs and makes instruments.
    Plays Caucasian tār. Lives in Mashhad.
31. Part-time musician from Mashhad, age ca. fifty; considered very good by
    his friends.

Violin:

32. Musician ca. forty-five, in Mashhad, also works as agent for musicians'
    groups; plays some western music as well as Persian.
33. Musician, ca. thirty, in Mashhad; performs in theater and is salesman of
    records and instruments; student of his father, but also studied from
    printed sources.
34. Musician in Mashhad, ca. thirty; studied in Tehran at Conservatory of
    National Music; teaches in private music studio and plays on radio.

Santour:

35. Music student, age ca. twenty-three, in Mashhad; born in Bojnurd;
    university student; teaches part-time in the school of the performer of
    Number 34.

Flute:

36. Amateur musician who is a civil servant, age ca. thirty, in Mashhad.

From published radif of chahārgāh (used only in analysis of thematic materials
given in Tables III, IV, V, and VI):

37. Hormoz Farhat, The Dastgāh Concept in Persian Classical Music.
    Unpublished dissertation, UCLA, 1966. p. 329.
38. From Musa Ma'arouffi's radif in Mehdi Berkechli, La musique
    traditionelle de l'Iran. Tehran, 1963. Transcriptions of chahārgāh pp. 1-4.
39. Abolhassan Saba. Radif: Dure-ye Sevvom-e Santur. (Tehran, 1958 [1337])
    pp. 31-32.
40a. Abolhassan Saba. Radif: Dure-ye Avval-e Violon.
    Sixth printing. (Tehran, 1965 [1344]) p. 40
40b. Abolhassan Saba. Radif: Dure-ye Dovvom-e Violon.
    Fourth printing. (Tehran, 1967 [1346]) p. 46

Table II.

Performances of Chahārgāh: Distribution and Order of Gushehā, and Length of Darāmadhā and Performances.

Performance			Timing (sec.)		Gusheh										
Type	Instrument	Number	Darāmad	Entire performance	Darāmad	Zābol	Hesār	Mokhalef	Maqlub	Hodi	Rajaz	Mansuri	Muyye	Other	Tape #
Teaching versions	setār	*1a	182	1512	1	2	3	4	6	8	10	11	7	Baste Negar 5 Pahlavi 9	24
	voice	2	141	944	1	3	4	5	6	8	2	7			16
Solo performances (Tehran)	setār	3	122	593	1	2	3								14
		4	180	354	1	2		3							*
		5	360	764	1	2	3	4							10
	tār	6	112	591	1	2	3	4				5			7
		7	60	294	1	2		3							*
	santur	8	140	600	1	2		3							3
		9	150	615	1	2	3	4							*
		10	153	900	2	3		1				5		Hozān 4	7
		11	280	1116	1	3	2	4							9
	violin	12	365	2040	1	2	4	3	5			6			4
		13	372	2133	1	2	4	5				6	3		5
		14	—	1039		2	6	5	3	1				Yati Maq. 4	26
		15	193	831	1	2	5	4					3		9
	kamānge	16	70	981	1	2		4					3		1
		17	282	960	1						4	5		Rak-e Abdallah 2 Chaharbeyti 3	10
		18	139	364	1	2									*
	nai	19b	58	311	1	2	6	4	5			7	3		22
	piano	20	79	255	1	2		3	4						11
Ensemble performances (Tehran)		21	143	755	1	2		3							*
		22	125	1688	1	2		3					4		14
		23	300	1095	1	2	3	4				5			15
		24	41	1105	1	2	4	3				5			11
		25	—	835	1	2									12
		26	—	2595		1		3					2		13
		27	270	1470	3	1	2								12
		28	86	1220	1	2	3	4	5			6			15
Performances in Khorasān	tār	29	155	360	1	2		3				4	5		25
		30	164	760	1	2		3							33
		31	30	258	1										28
	violin	32	135	778	1	2		3							26
		33	98	572	1	2	4	3				5			27
		34	57	345	1	2									26
	santur	35	141	250	1		2								27
	flute	36	146	254	1	2		3							27

*Commercial.

No. 25 is performed entirely in the metric "zarbi" style; it is impossible to indicate the point of transition precisely.

46

Table III

Darāmad of Chahārgāh: Themes and Thematic Motifs

ZEB BILLINGS
MUSIC PUBLISHING COMPANY
A DIVISION OF PROGRAMED SYSTEMS, INC.
6056 W. Fond du Lac Ave. Milwaukee, Wis. 53218

Darāmad of chahārgāh : themes and thematic motifs
(Continued)

XI ... 16

XII ... 196

ZEB BILLINGS
MUSIC PUBLISHING COMPANY
A DIVISION OF PROGRAMMED SYSTEMS, INC.
8055 W. Fond du Lac Ave. Milwaukee, Wis. 53218

Table IV

Categories of Performances; Number of Darāmads and Unit Subdivisions

Type of performance	No. of darāmad performances	Total number of units in darāmad performances
Teaching versions	9	20
Solo performances (Tehran)	17	42
Ensemble performances (Tehran)	6	14
Performances in Khorasan	8	13
TOTAL	40	89

Table V

Categories of Performances: Distribution of Themes

Type of performance	Themes											
	I	VIII	VI	VII	IV	III	XI	II	X	V	IX	XII
Teaching	9	9	9	4	4	3	2	2	2	2	1	0
Solo	17	12	11	8	2	10	8	8	5	2	1	1
Ensemble	6	5	3	6	0	1	3	1	1	0	1	0
from Khorasan	7	6	0	5	0	4	6	3	1	1	0	0
TOTAL	39	32	23	23	6	18	19	14	9	5	3	1

49

Table VI.

Darāmad of Chahārgāh: Distribution and Order of Themes and Thematic Motifs.

	I	II	III	IV	V	VI	VII	VIII	IX	X	XI	XII	Comments
1a	1, 4					2		3					First darāmad
	1, 4					2		3					Second darāmad
	1, 4		2					3					Kereshmeh
1b	1, 3					2							First darāmad
	1, 5	2	3					4					Second darāmad
	1, 6			3				5	2		4		Zangouleh
	1, 5, 7		6			2	3	4					Fourth darāmad
2	1, 4					2		3					
	5, 7							6					
	13		10				8	12	9, 11				
3	1				4			3, 6			2, 5		
	7							9		8			
4	1, 3							2					
	4							5					
	6	8						7					
	9, 12							11		10			
5	1, 3		2										
	4, 8		6			5		7					Darāmad
	9		12		10						11		
	1, 3		2										Kereshmeh
				3					1		2, 4		Zangouleh
6	1, 3					2							
	4, 6					5							
	11							8, 10	7, 9				
7	1, 3					2							
	4, 7					5	6						
8	1, 4, 7	6	2				3			5			
9	1, 3	4				2		5					
								7	6				
10	1	2						3					
	4					5	6	8		7			
11	1, 4, 6		3, 5			2	7						plus zarbi
12	1, 3					2							
	4, 8	5	6					7					
	9, 14	10	13							12	11		
	15, 19		18		16					17			
13	1, 3					2							First darāmad
	4, 7	5	6										
	2						1						Second darāmad
	1, 5	2	3							4			Return to the
	9		7				6				8		first darāmad
14													
15	1, 5, 7		3			2	4	6					First darāmad
	1, 6		3, 5				4				2		second darāmad
16	1, 4	2						3					
			5					6					

	I	II	III	IV	V	VI	VII	VIII	IX	X	XI	XII	Comments
17	1,6,8,11	2	4, 9				5	3, 7, 10					
18	1, 3							2					
	4		5				6	7					
19a	1, 5						4				2	3	*Improvisation*
	6										7	8	*on the darāmad*
	10, 12						9				11		
19b	1, 3, 6					2	4	5					
20	1, 4, 6		3			2, 5							
21	1					3		5			2, 4		
								7			6		
22	11		8				9	10					
	1							3			2		
	6						5			4			
23	1, 4					2		3					
	5, 8						6	7					
24	1, 3, 6						2, 5				4		
25													
26													
27	1, 5					2	3	4					
	6, 9					7	8						
	10, 14	11					12	13					
	20	15,17					16	19	18				
28	1, 4						2	3					
	5, 7							6					
29	1, 3, 5		2, 4										
	6, 9, 12						7	8, 11			10		
	15		13					14					
30	1, 3							2					
	4, 6				5								
	10, 13						8, 11	7, 9, 12					
31	2, 6, 9		7					1, 3,5,8			4		
32	3, 6	1, 5						2			4		
33	1									3	2		
	4	7					6			8	5		
34	1, 4						3				2		
35			5				3, 6	1, 4, 7			2		
36	1,3,6,8	2	4					5, 7					
37	1, 4					2		3					
38	1, 4					2		3					*First darāmad*
	1, 4	2	3										*Second darāmad*
	1, 4		3			2							*Third darāmad*
	1				2						3		*Fourth darāmad*
39	1, 3					2							
	4, 9		5, 7				6	8					
40a	1,3,4,8			7		2		5		6			
40b	1,3,4,7	5				2		6					

51

THE TRANSCRIPTIONS

TRANSCRIPTIONS OF fifteen performances of the daramad of chahārgāh discussed in this study are included. These are in no way intended to aid performance or to provide a complete visual record of the sound. They do not contain very much of the ornamentation, nor is there an attempt, in the non-metric sections, to provide precise measurement of note-lengths and their proportions. They are approximations, which may help the reader to understand the over-all structure and the relationship of sections to each other. It must be remembered that long notes should usually be interpreted as tremolos (riz) when performed on santour, setar, or tar. Fine variations in pitch are not indicated, although these are frequent in Persian classical music, especially variations in the size of the three-quarter and five-quarter tones. Larger deviations from the scale of chahārgāh are indicated, as in the case of the "modulation" to Hesār in Performance Number 11. All transcriptions are transposed to c, but the original tonic is given at the head of each transcription. Only major changes in tempo and dynamics are indicated. However, it must be remembered that characteristically the phrasing in Persian classical music is accompanied by swells in tempo and dynamics, and that the non-metric materials are exceedingly difficult to represent in western, meter-oriented notation. In order to aid the reader we have used "time-space" notation, where each line of transcription comprises ten seconds of music and is divided into two equally spaced five-second segments. This should provide some indication of tempo and rhythmic activity. Structural subdivisions within a performance are indicated by letters, and themes are designated by Roman numerals as given in Tables III and VI.

Darāmad #2 (voice)
"Darāmad" and "tahrīr" sections have no text

ZEB BILLINGS
MUSIC PUBLISHING COMPANY
A DIVISION OF PROGRAMMED SYSTEMS, INC.
8055 W. Fond du Lac Ave. Milwaukee, Wis. 53218

Darāmad # 2 (voice) (Continued)

ZEB BILLINGS
MUSIC PUBLISHING COMPANY
A DIVISION OF PROGRAMMED SYSTEMS, INC.
6055 W. Fond du Lac Ave. Milwaukee, Wis. 53218

Darāmad #3 (setār)

ZEB BILLINGS
MUSIC PUBLISHING COMPANY
A DIVISION OF PROGRAMMED SYSTEMS, INC.
6055 W. Fond du Lac Ave, Milwaukee, Wis. 53218

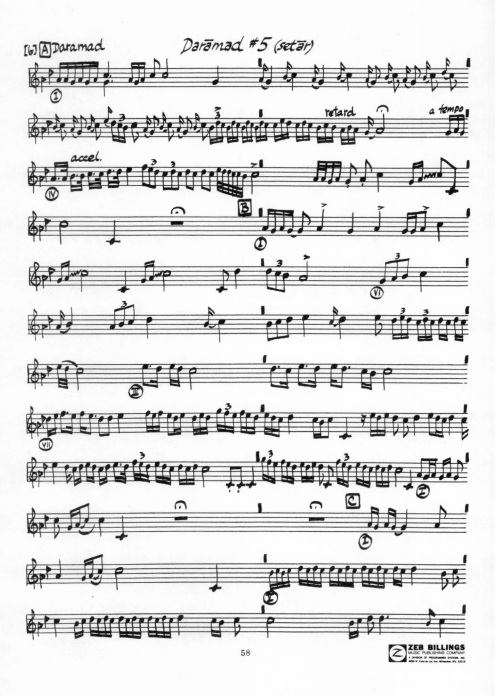

Darāmad #5 (setār)

ZEB BILLINGS
MUSIC PUBLISHING COMPANY
A DIVISION OF PROGRAMMED SYSTEMS, INC.
6095 W. Fond du Lac Ave. Milwaukee, Wis. 53218

Kereshmeh

begins gradually to be less zarbi

59

Darāmad #5 (setār) (Continued)

ZEB BILLINGS
MUSIC PUBLISHING COMPANY
A DIVISION OF PROGRAMMED SYSTEMS, INC.
6095 W. Fond du Lac Ave. Milwaukee, Wis. 53218

Darāmad #6 (tār)

ZEB BILLINGS
MUSIC PUBLISHING COMPANY
A DIVISION OF PROGRAMMED SYSTEMS, INC.
6095 W. Fond du Lac Ave Milwaukee, Wis. 53218

Darāmad #7 (tār)

ZEB BILLINGS
MUSIC PUBLISHING COMPANY
A DIVISION OF PROGRAMMED SYSTEMS, INC.
6066 W. Fond du Lac Ave. Milwaukee, Wis. 53218

Darāmad #10 (santour)

ZEB BILLINGS
MUSIC PUBLISHING COMPANY
A DIVISION OF PROGRAMMED SYSTEMS, INC.
8055 W. Fond du Lac Ave. Milwaukee, Wis. 53218

Darāmad #10 (santour) (Continued)

single stroke pp

ZEB BILLINGS
MUSIC PUBLISHING COMPANY
A DIVISION OF PROGRAMMED SYSTEMS, INC.
6056 W. Fond du Lac Ave. Milwaukee, Wis. 53218

[a]

Darāmad #11 (santour)

ZEB BILLINGS
MUSIC PUBLISHING COMPANY
A DIVISION OF PROGRAMMED SYSTEMS, INC.
8055 W. Fond du Lac Ave. Milwaukee, Wis. 53218

Darāmad #11 (santour) (Continued)

Daramad #12 (violin)

ZEB BILLINGS
MUSIC PUBLISHING COMPANY
A DIVISION OF PROGRAMMED SYSTEMS, INC.
8055 W. Fond du Lac Ave. Milwaukee, Wis. 53218

Darāmad #12 (violin) (Continued)

ZEB BILLINGS
MUSIC PUBLISHING COMPANY
A DIVISION OF PROGRAMMED SYSTEMS, INC.
6095 W. Fond du Lac Ave. Milwaukee, WI. 53218

69

Daramad #13 (violin)

71

Darāmad #13 (violin) (Continued)

ZEB BILLINGS
MUSIC PUBLISHING COMPANY
A DIVISION OF PROGRAMMED SYSTEMS, INC.
6055 W. Fond du Lac Ave. Milwaukee, Wis. 53218

ZEB BILLINGS
MUSIC PUBLISHING COMPANY
A DIVISION OF PROGRAMMED SYSTEMS, INC.
9255 W. Fond du Lac Ave. Milwaukee, Wis. 53218

Darāmad #15 (violin)

ZEB BILLINGS
MUSIC PUBLISHING COMPANY
A DIVISION OF PROGRAMMED SYSTEMS, INC.
6065 W. Fond du Lac Ave. Milwaukee, Wis. 53218

ZEB BILLINGS
MUSIC PUBLISHING COMPANY
A DIVISION OF PROGRAMMED SYSTEMS, INC.
6055 W. Fond du Lac Ave. Milwaukee, Wis. 53218

Darāmad #16 (kamāngé)

ZEB BILLINGS
MUSIC PUBLISHING COMPANY
A DIVISION OF PROGRAMMED SYSTEMS, INC.
8055 W. Fond du Lac Ave. Milwaukee, Wis. 53218

Darāmad #19a (nai)

ZEB BILLINGS
MUSIC PUBLISHING COMPANY
A DIVISION OF PROGRAMMED SYSTEMS, INC.
6055 W. Fond du Lac Ave. Milwaukee, Wis. 53216

Darāmad #19a (nai) (Continued)

ZEB BILLINGS
MUSIC PUBLISHING COMPANY
A DIVISION OF PROGRAMED SYSTEMS, INC.
6055 W. Fond du Lac Ave. Milwaukee, Wis. 53218

ZEB BILLINGS
MUSIC PUBLISHING COMPANY
A DIVISION OF PROGRAMMED SYSTEMS, INC.
6055 W. Fond du Lac Ave. Milwaukee, Wis. 53218

Darāmad #22 (voice and nai)

ZEB BILLINGS
MUSIC PUBLISHING COMPANY
A DIVISION OF PROGRAMMED SYSTEMS, INC.
6085 W. Fond du Lac Ave. Milwaukee, Wis. 53218

[nai not audible]

81

Darāmad #28 (voice)

ZEB BILLINGS
MUSIC PUBLISHING COMPANY
A DIVISION OF PROGRAMMED SYSTEMS, INC.
6055 W. Fond du Lac Ave. Milwaukee, Wis. 53218

ZEB BILLINGS
MUSIC PUBLISHING COMPANY
A DIVISION OF PROGRAMMED SYSTEMS, INC.
8055 W. Fond du Lac Ave. Milwaukee, WI. 53218

Darāmad #33 (violin)

ZEB BILLINGS
MUSIC PUBLISHING COMPANY
A DIVISION OF PROGRAMMED SYSTEMS, INC.
8055 W. Fond du Lac Ave. Milwaukee, WI. 53218

DETROIT MONOGRAPHS IN MUSICOLOGY

This new series of musicological studies includes historical, ethnomusicological and theoretical materials.

Editorial Committee
Albert Cohen
   State University of New York at Buffalo
Bruno Nettl
   University of Illinois at Urbana-Champaign
Howard Smither
   University of North Carolina

THE BEGINNINGS OF MUSICAL NATIONALISM IN BRAZIL,
   by Gerard Behague 1971 43p $5.00   Number 1

DETROIT STUDIES IN MUSIC BIBLIOGRAPHY
.... Bruno Nettl, General Editor

REFERENCE MATERIALS IN ETHNOMUSICOLOGY, by
   Bruno Nettl Rev ed 1967 40p $2.00   Number 1

SIR ARTHUR SULLIVAN: AN INDEX TO THE TEXTS OF
   HIS VOCAL WORKS, compiled by Sirvart Poladian
   1961 91p $2.75   Number 2

AN INDEX TO BEETHOVEN'S CONVERSATION BOOKS, by
   Donald W. MacArdle 1962 46p $2.00   Number 3

GENERAL BIBLIOGRAPHY FOR MUSIC RESEARCH, by
   Keith E. Mixter 1962 38p $2.00   Number 4

A HANDBOOK OF AMERICAN OPERATIC PREMIERES,
   1731-1962, by Julius Mattfeld 1963 142p $3.00   Number 5

MEDIEVAL AND RENAISSANCE MUSIC ON LONG-PLAYING
   RECORDS, by James Coover and Richard Colvig 1964
   122p $3.00   Number 6

RHODE ISLAND MUSIC AND MUSICIANS, 1733-1850, by
   Joyce Ellen Mangler 1965 90p $2.75   Number 7

DETROIT STUDIES IN MUSIC BIBLIOGRAPHY

.... Bruno Nettl, General Editor